Puffin Books
Editor: Kaye Webb

The Birthday Unicorn

Alexander Columbus Banyana lived in a little house on top of the famous Ritz-Palace hotel. He had a daring explorer father, who wore a curly black moustache, and a dashing, famous mother who wrote books and travelled in her own little aeroplane or else in a pink mini car covered in daisies.

They were pretty unusual people, the Banyanas, and Alexander was fairly used to surprises, but even he was amazed when his father sent him two big birthday packing cases from the depths of the Amazonian jungle, and they turned out to contain a Unicorn and a Dodo, both alive, kicking and full of character.

'It is the most wonderful present I have ever had in the WHOLE of my life!' said Alexander. And he was right, for the Unicorn and the Dodo were to be his companions in some of the most exciting and dangerous (and funny) experiences he had ever had.

Janice Elliott is a well-known adult novelist, but this delicious fantasy is her first book for children.

For readers of eight and over.

Janice Elliott

The Birthday Unicorn

Illustrated by Michael Foreman

uffin Books

Puffin Books, Penguin Books Ltd, Harmondsworth,
Middlesex, England
Penguin Books, 625 Madison Avenue,
New York, New York 10022, U.S.A.
Penguin Books Australia Ltd, Ringwood,
Victoria, Australia
Penguin Books Canada Ltd, 2801 John Street,
Markham, Ontario, Canada L3R 1B4
Penguin Books (N.Z.) Ltd, 182–190 Wairau Road,
Auckland 10, New Zealand

First published by Victor Gollancz 1970
Published in Puffin Books 1973
Reprinted 1977

Copyright © Janice Elliott, 1970
Illustrations copyright © Michael Foreman, 1970
All rights reserved

Made and printed in Great Britain by
Richard Clay (The Chaucer Press) Ltd
Bungay, Suffolk
Set in Monotype Garamond

For Alexander Cooper

I

Alexander Columbus Banyana had red hair and lived with his parents in a small house on top of the famous Ritz-Palace hotel. You could not see this house even from a big London bus and very few people knew it was there. It had its own private lift and a staircase from outside. If you could find the door you might have seen a very small notice made of brass which read:

MR AND MRS BANYANA
AND ALEXANDER

Mr Banyana said this was a good place to live because it was central and he could land his red helicopter on the flat roof. The Banyanas used to have an enormous car with a chauffeur called William. Then there were too many cars in London so William took Alexander to school every morning on a tandem bicycle.
William liked the bicycle better than the car,

and to ride it he wore a peaked cap and a striped sweater in purple and white. Mrs Banyana knitted this for him. William was a great friend of the Banyanas and for her birthday he painted Mrs Banyana's pink mini car all over with daisies. She drove this very fast, but only in the afternoons, because she did not get up till twelve o'clock. She was very beautiful and famous and wrote books into which she put William's remarks.

Mr Banyana was an explorer. He was tall and handsome and wore a curly black moustache and a solar topee. Before Alexander had to go to school he used to travel with his mother and William on Mr Banyana's adventures. They must have made a fine sight, riding on camels or donkeys or bicycles, depending upon where they were trying to discover. Mr Banyana rode in front wearing his solar topee, William at the back in his striped sweater and in the middle Mrs Banyana and Alexander. In India Alexander slept on a silk cushion in a howdah. At the south pole he travelled on his own small sledge in a fur bag, with only his nose sticking out. Wherever they went he always wore a strong luggage label which read:

THIS IS
ALEXANDER COLUMBUS
BANYANA.
IF FOUND PLEASE RETURN TO
MR AND MRS BANYANA,
THE FAMOUS RITZ-PALACE HOTEL,
LONDON.

After school William often took Alexander to Islington to have tea with his sister, Lily. She smelled nice and looked like two round cottage loaves on top of each other. She gave William Madeira cake and dark brown tea. Meanwhile the tabby cat, just as round as Lily, had a saucer of sweetened condensed milk, and Alexander ate his special tea. This was always the same: sardines on toast, Welsh rarebit and celery. Alexander did not like sweet things and Lily was the only grown-up, apart from William, who understood this.

One day Alexander was having tea with Lily and William in Islington. They had just finished and William was smoking his cigar while the cat cleaned the sweetened condensed milk off its whiskers. Lily knitted some red socks for

Mr Banyana ready for the next time he decided to go to the south pole.

'Well,' said Lily, comfortably, 'so it's your birthday soon.'

'Yes,' said Alexander, 'in five and a half days.'

'That's nice then.'

Alexander looked rather sad. He could never pretend with Lily and William, and he was rather afraid he might cry when William asked:

'What's up, old mate?'

Lily knew. She turned a heel and said:

'He misses his Dad.'

Alexander cried a bit. Lily kissed him and said, 'There, there.' She asked William: 'Where is he this year?'

'In the depths of the Amazonian jungle.'

Mr Banyana was good and kind and brave and modest. He loved his son and Alexander was proud of him, as he was of both his parents. When Mr Banyana came home once a year, landing on the roof in his red helicopter, Alexander thought he would burst. Mr Banyana had only one weakness: he forgot

Alexander's birthday. When Alexander was

five Mr Banyana was fighting off desperate warring Kurdish tribesmen single-handed. When his son was six, he was discovering a previously unknown and extremely fierce blood-sucking horse fly in a filthy malarial swamp somewhere off the Nile. Mr Banyana was so excited that he forgot to eat for several days and nearly sank.

Lily said: 'He ought to remember birthdays.'

'Well,' said William, 'he has a lot on his mind.'

'Birthday presents are more important than anything,' said Lily fiercely. Alexander had never seen her like this. Buster the cat stopped cleaning its whiskers. William stood to attention. 'William!' said Lily. 'Something must be done!'

That evening William had a long talk with Mrs Banyana. When they had finished, Mrs Banyana, who seemed vague but underneath was very determined and businesslike, came in to see Alexander in bed. She was wearing something beautiful and orange and had dyed her hair to match. Every night she came in wearing diamonds or rubies and, sometimes, a small 12 crown on her head, to tell Alexander a story. Tonight she seemed very serious.

'It is your birthday,' she said, 'in about five and a quarter days. William and I have decided that your father must be told. I shall fly tomorrow to the depths of the Amazonian jungle.'

Alexander knew that his mother sometimes exaggerated and that she could not possibly fly all the way. There are a lot of trees in the Amazonian jungle, so she would have to walk part of the way and then take a canoe. But he had no doubt that she would get there and back in five and a quarter days.

In the morning she drove to the airfield in her pink mini car. Alexander and William went to see her off. Her private aeroplane was waiting, spreading its silver wings in the sunshine. She kissed Alexander and shook hands with William. She put on her flying helmet and turned at the top of the steps to wave.

'I shall be back,' she said, 'at six o'clock in four and a half days. And I shall bring a birthday present from your father.'

2

While Mrs Banyana was away looking for his father in the depths of the Amazonian jungle, Alexander received two telegrams. Mrs Banyana never wrote letters or used the telephone, but she often sent telegrams. They were always very long or very short.

When she was at home Mrs Banyana was good at remembering important things. She never forgot a birthday or a picnic or a promise to take Alexander to Paris for tea in her aeroplane. But she did overlook details. Alexander had once gone to Islington in bare feet when his shoes wore out. The trouble was that although Mrs Banyana was very fond of Alexander and thought he was intelligent and kind, she only noticed twice a year that he was growing. Then she would look at him and say: 'You are growing.' Lily said: 'Tchk, tchk,' and sent William out to buy shoes and socks and string vests. Alexander did not mind too much because his mother was always full of surprises, and he would rather have surprises than socks.

Sometimes when Mrs Banyana was away, she would suddenly remember that Alexander was growing, so he was not surprised when the first telegram said:

SYDNEY PROCEED AT ONCE OXFORD STREET BUY PYJAMAS

Alexander and William were having breakfast together when the telegram arrived. William had cooked porridge, kidneys, eggs, bacon and tomatoes.

'I understand about the pyjamas,' said Alexander, 'but who is Sydney? My name is Alexander.'

William did not like to be spoken to when he was having his breakfast. It was the only time in the day, Alexander noticed, when he was not quite ready for a chat. But he put on his reading glasses and looked at the telegram.

15   'Well?' said Alexander.

'It means,' said William, 'that she has gone round the other way.'

'But there's only one way to the depths of the Amazonian jungle.'

William sighed and put down his fork.

'Since the world is round,' he said, 'if you go up in the air and turn right instead of left you will still, if you so wish, arrive in the depths of the Amazonian jungle. She sent the telegram from Australia.'

'But who's Sydney?'

'Sydney is either a kangaroo or a place in Australia. Look it up.'

'Oh,' said Alexander.

The next telegram said:

I THOUGHT I WOULD GO ROUND THE OTHER WAY FOR A CHANGE

'I told you,' said William.

At exactly six o'clock on Alexander's birthday Mrs Banyana arrived, still wearing her flying helmet. She had left her pink mini car right in the middle of Piccadilly and all the red buses and taxis and cars were swerving and hooting and pulling terrible faces as they tried

to get round it. A policeman was guarding the mini car because it was Mrs Banyana's.

Without bothering to take off her flying helmet Mrs Banyana kissed Alexander and said:

'Today is your birthday. I found your father in a jungle clearing among hostile natives. He is very well and sends his love. I have brought you a surprise and it should arrive momentarily.'

Just then the lift purred and the gates opened. Two policemen, three under-porters, one bell boy and the Manager of the famous Ritz-Palace hotel emerged, rather red in the face and panting behind two large packing cases with holes in the side. One was making a peculiar noise, like crying, and there was a sound of stamping in the other. William got a crowbar and with the two policemen, the three under-porters, the bell boy and the Manager, succeeded in prising open the boxes. Out of one stepped a white horse with a horn on its forehead, stamping and blowing steam. Alexander recognized it immediately.

'It's a Unicorn!'

'There's no such thing,' said William, boggling and mopping his brow.

The second box contained a large bird with very short wings. It had a nice face but it was crying. It walked rather awkwardly out of the box and crashed into a priceless Chinese vase.

Mrs Banyana was drinking champagne.

'Didus ineptus,' she said.

William looked suspicious. He thought he'd seen everything in his time.

'And what's that when it's at home?'

'Dodo.'

'But that's extinct.'

'Mostly.'

'Well,' said William, 'wonders will never cease.'

Alexander stroked the Unicorn and mopped up the Dodo's tears with his handkerchief. He looked round at his mother and William. He looked at the two policemen, three under-porters, one bell boy and the Manager of the famous Ritz-Palace hotel, and said:

'It is the most wonderful present I have ever had in the WHOLE of my life!'

3

The morning after Alexander's birthday he was afraid it might all have been a dream and would finish when he woke up. But then he heard the Dodo snore and the Unicorn stamp, and he opened his eyes.

'I thought you would never wake up,' the Unicorn said. It had a soft, musical voice, but looked rather cross. It poked the Dodo with its hoof. The Dodo stopped in the middle of a snore, just like William on Sunday afternoons when he had had Lily's roast beef, Yorkshire pudding and apple pie for lunch. It brought out its head from under its wing, blinked and put it back.

Alexander said: 'Shouldn't we let it sleep?' He was not sure how to address a Unicorn.

'You may call me Your Grace,' said the Unicorn. 'Because I'm very graceful.' He shook his mane and looked in the mirror. 'The

Dodo on the other hand is clumsy. That's why it's extinct.'

In the afternoon Alexander and William took the Unicorn and the Dodo to see Lily.

William said: 'She'll never believe it.'

Mrs Banyana said: 'You may borrow my pink mini car because the most famous photographer in the whole world is coming to take a picture of me.'

The Unicorn took the lift very calmly, but when they got to the bottom the Dodo, who seemed rather short-sighted, perhaps because his eyes were always filled with tears, tried to get out before the doors were open. He banged his beak.

As it was Sunday afternoon Piccadilly was almost empty. Mrs Banyana's pink mini car was still parked in the middle of the road. The same policeman was guarding it, because no one had told him to stop. He saluted Alexander and William, then he saw the Unicorn and the Dodo. His mouth opened wide, he rubbed his eyes and his helmet fell off.

The Unicorn sat in front by William, his
head sticking through the sun roof. The Dodo

sat in the back with Alexander and went to sleep. When they got to Lily's they had to wake him up.

Lily had laid out an extra special tea because it was the day after Alexander's birthday. When it saw the Dodo and the Unicorn, her fat cat, Buster, screamed, stood all its coat on end so that it looked like a soft porcupine and jumped on to Lily's shoulder.

Alexander said: 'My father sent them for my birthday. It was the best present I have ever had in the whole of my life.'

They had tea. Lily had taken the Dodo and the Unicorn very calmly. When they asked her if she wasn't surprised, she said:

'I believe what I see. And sometimes, if I try, I see what I believe.'

'I'm mythical,' said the Unicorn, who was eating celery.

'I'm extinct,' said the Dodo, and burst into tears.

'There, there,' said Lily.

'And what's more, I can't fly.'

'Never you mind,' said Lily. 'Neither can I.'

The Dodo cheered up and drank some tea. It seemed to like Lily. Buster flattened his fur

coat and tried to look thin and dangerous, but no one took any notice. He stalked the Dodo once or twice, then gave up and climbed on Lily's lap.

When they left Lily kissed Alexander and the Dodo and shook hands with the Unicorn. It had been a nice afternoon.

They were very cheerful driving back, as if they'd been to a party. The Unicorn, who was still putting on airs, but was more sociable, told them how he had been born before the world began and seen the earth made and the stars and the sun and the moon put in the sky. And Man was made and hunted him, so for hundreds and thousands and millions of years he had hidden until he heard them say: 'There is no such thing as a Unicorn, so we cannot catch him.' Then he walked around the world for a while but no one saw him till one morning, in the quiet green clearing, a tall Man arrived, wearing a curly black moustache and a solar topee.

'That's my father!' said Alexander.

'I would thank you,' said the Unicorn, 'not to interrupt.'

'I'm sorry,' said Alexander. 'Please go on.'

'I'd finished anyway.'

The Dodo, who had been quiet all this time, began to sing, in a queer little breaking voice.

'I am a bird that cannot fly
So the only thing
Is to sing
What is a bird without wings?
What am I?'

'I think you're very nice,' said Alexander.

'Thank you,' said the Dodo. 'All I have is my voice.' The Unicorn sniffed.

William said: 'Hello, hello! What's going on?'

They had driven through the empty streets, taking a long cut past London's river. They had reached Piccadilly Circus.

'It doesn't rhyme,' said the Unicorn, 'thing and wings.'

While the Dodo and the Unicorn were arguing, Alexander and William noticed that a crowd had collected, filling all the pavement and the road from Leicester Square to the Ritz-Palace hotel.

Alexander said: 'My mother must have written another book.'

Then, spotting the pink mini car, the crowd began to roar and cheer and surge forward. There was great danger that the mini car might be overturned. William said:

'That policeman must have told his wife who told her sister who told the papers.' He mopped his brow with a red spotted handkerchief he had worn to keep off mosquitoes in the malarial swamps of the lower Nile.

Faces were pressing against the windscreen and photographers were flashing their bulbs. The Unicorn waved a hoof, like the Queen, and gave them his best profile. The Dodo was muttering to himself: 'It does rhyme, it *does*.'

Someone pushed a microphone into the sun roof. The Unicorn said:

'I'd rather be mythical than extinct.'

The Dodo cried again. Just as they were about to be crushed the crowd fell back. The Manager of the Ritz-Palace hotel stood in the middle of the road in a tail-coat and a top hat. A helicopter circled overhead. The Unicorn bowed politely out of the sun roof as William steered the car to the back door. Someone threw a carnation and the Unicorn caught it in his teeth.

26

William said: 'You're famous now.'

As they ran for the door the Dodo was heard faintly to remark:

'I don't *care* if it rhymes or not. It's *my* song.'

While William was trying to push them all into the lift, the Unicorn was posing for photographs.

Alexander remarked to William:

'I never thought we'd be famous.'

At last the Unicorn came in. His mane was ruffled and he had dropped his carnation, but he looked pleased.

'*Such* nice people.'

'Come on,' said Alexander. 'It's time to go to bed.'

The Dodo was already asleep, but from time to time it opened its beak and murmured:

'What is a bird without wings?
What am I?'

'He does go on,' said the Unicorn. Then they all went to bed.

4

Everyone at the Ritz-Palace hotel was very
nice to the Unicorn and the Dodo. Even the
Manager, who was a very important person,
came up every morning to ask how they were.
Alphonse, the head-waiter, sent up trays of
celery and rose water for the Unicorn and nuts
for the Dodo. The staff clubbed together to
buy a mirror for the Unicorn, who was rather
vain. And a little silver bell for the Dodo to
hang round his neck. This was in case he fell
over and couldn't get up, or got lost because
he couldn't see where he was going. They had
a presentation for them in the big ballroom.
They all wore their best uniforms and the
Manager wore his tail-coat but not his top hat,
because that would not be polite indoors. The
Unicorn made a long speech, and the Dodo
went to sleep. Then they all sang: 'For They

are Jolly Good Fellows' and the Dodo woke up and rang his bell.

Mrs Banyana said the Unicorn and the Dodo must never, *never* go out of doors without Alexander or William or they might get stolen or put in a Zoo. The day they had such a scare coming home through the crowds from Lily's, Mrs Banyana had been marvellous. She had put on her best gold dress and a small crown and gone out on to the balcony outside the Manager's office, to address the crowd. Quite soon they had gone away and now when they went out there were only a few knots of people cheering and throwing flowers. Though the newspapers and television kept ringing up and sending telegrams and trying to get into the Ritz-Palace hotel in disguise.

Mrs Banyana said: 'No comment.'

William said: 'It's a nine-day wonder.'

Alexander asked: 'What's a nine-day wonder?'

'Look it up,' said William.

The Unicorn looked at the *Daily Telegraph* and said: 'That's not my best profile.' He shook his head in a temper and went to look in a
mirror.

The papers said:

HORNED HORSE
FOXES EXPERTS

and in smaller letters:

GIANT OWL AT RITZ-PALACE HOTEL

'Horse!' said the Unicorn, and stamped his foot. 'I could turn them into TOADS!'

The Dodo said nothing. It had been very depressed since they got back from Lily's and Alexander guessed it was because everyone, except Lily, seemed to like the Unicorn best. The Unicorn's picture was always biggest in the paper and everyone made jokes about the Dodo. The Dodo could not turn anyone into a toad. The Unicorn could play chess and make speeches. One day, when Alexander took them both to school, it gave a whole geography lesson and afterwards the teacher shook hands with it and it did some magic. It knew more than William and could talk about everything in the world, even before the world began. When they went out to walk in the Park before breakfast, before the newspapers and the television got up, even the birds laughed at the

Dodo, though they were very respectful to the Unicorn.

One day a Mr Simon Anstruther-Pettigrew-Pringle rang up. He was the most famous television interviewer in the whole world and even Mrs Banyana's friend, the Prime Minister, was frightened of him.

He said: 'I shall send round a car to take Alexander and William and the Dodo and the Unicorn to the television studios at Shepherd's Bush at six o'clock exactly.' Then, before Mrs Banyana could open her mouth to say 'No comment', he rang off. The Unicorn said in a casual sort of voice that he didn't mind. The Dodo was asleep in the airing cupboard. Alexander thought it was rather exciting. William put on his best purple and white striped sweater. The Unicorn polished his horn and set his mane in curlers.

At six o'clock exactly the car arrived. William sat in front with the Unicorn and the driver. In the back Alexander held the Dodo's wing. He wished he could do magic to make the Dodo happy.

Mr Simon Anstruther-Pettigrew-Pringle was

very thin and sarcastic. He wore a blue velvet suit and a pink-spotted tie. Alexander thought Lily would say he wanted feeding up. While they were waiting to go on they drank fizzy orange squash. The Dodo ate a nut and had a dreadful coughing fit. William, who was not going on, thumped it on the back and it fell over. The Unicorn sighed.

Mr Simon Anstruther-Pettigrew-Pringle was very nice at first. Alexander explained about his birthday present. The Unicorn crossed its hoofs and smiled into the camera. It took no notice of Mr Simon Anstruther-Pettigrew-Pringle's questions but said it was very, *very* happy to be there.

Mr Simon Anstruther-Pettigrew-Pringle said in a sarcastic sort of voice:

'Perhaps you would tell us, in your own words, how old you are?'

'A thousand million billion years,' said the Unicorn. The studio audience clapped politely.

'I'm sorry,' said Mr Simon Anstruther-Pettigrew-Pringle, 'but I can't quite believe that.'

Just then the Dodo fell off its perch. There was a horrible crash and Alexander put it back. 32

'I put it to you,' said Mr Simon Anstruther-Pettigrew-Pringle, 'that there is no such thing. I put it to you that you are mythical and your friend is extinct!'

The Unicorn snorted with rage. A camera fell over and someone held up a notice saying

KINDLY DO NOT
ADJUST YOUR SET

Alexander held his breath. The Unicorn galloped off, turning several people into toads.

There was an awful silence. The producer began to cry. Mr Simon Anstruther-Pettigrew-Pringle tore his spotted tie into small pieces. The audience stamped their feet. Then the Dodo, who had been sitting quietly all this time, began to sing:

> 'If there's no such thing
> Then why
> Am I
> Who cannot fly?'

The studio audience roared and cheered. They rose to their feet. They threw flowers and nuts and lemon meringue pies at the Dodo who 34 smiled and bowed and spread his tiny wings in pride.

Outside, very late, long after Alexander's bed time, everyone wanted to shake the Dodo by the wing. He smiled, and cried a bit, and made a small speech, and said:

> 'It's quite absurd
> I'm only a bird.'

Alexander said: 'I knew you could be happy.'

The Unicorn sulked, then thought better of it and extended a hoof.

William said: 'It's time everyone went to bed.'

The Dodo fluffed out his feathers with happiness, and went to sleep.

5

After they had been on television the Dodo and
the Unicorn were very busy for a while. Everyone wrote to them or telephoned to say that
this was the best television programme they
had ever seen in the whole of their lives, and
please would they do it again? Mr Simon
Anstruther-Pettigrew-Pringle had gone on a
long holiday. Another interviewer, a very nice
person who said she *did* believe in Unicorns and
Dodos, kept ringing up to ask them to go on
again. And Alexander of course, because he
was quite famous too. But William put his foot
down and said:

'Enough is *enough*.' Mrs Banyana agreed.

They got so many letters that they had to
have a secretary who answered the telephone
and sent out photographs of the Dodo and the
Unicorn and Alexander. She also wrote letters
for the Unicorn (who had quite forgotten that   36

the Dodo had done best on television) to the Prime Minister, the Admiral of the Fleet and the Editor of *The Times*.

The Dodo was asked to join several pop groups as a singer, and the Beatles said if he would come and sing with them they would change their name to the Dodos. The Dodo was pleased but suddenly felt shy and went into the airing cupboard.

The Unicorn was rather awkward at first about turning the toads at the television centre back into people. Mrs Banyana and William and Alexander and the Dodo tried to persuade him. But he only agreed when Mr Banyana, who had left the depths of the Amazonian jungle and was thinking on top of a mountain in Tibet, sent a telegram:

IT IS NOT KIND TO TURN PEOPLE INTO TOADS

The people who had been turned back were very grateful and sent thank you letters.

The Unicorn spoke at the Albert Hall and did some tricks for the Magic Circle (after he had promised not to turn anyone into a toad).

He launched the biggest ship in the world and went for tea at the Palace.

William said: 'The Unicorn is getting airs.'

As they became even more famous the Unicorn got vainer and vainer and the Dodo shyer and shyer, until it was spending most of the day in the airing cupboard. One day when the Unicorn was giving a small party in the ballroom for about two hundred or so, William came in and said in a terrible voice:

'Enough is ENOUGH.'

The people went away. The secretary admitmitted she was very tired and went downstairs to marry the under-manager. After a while the telephone stopped ringing and the letters stopped coming. Alexander went to bed at the proper time. The Dodo came out from the airing cupboard and rang its bell. They could all go out in the streets and the shops and people hardly took a second look. The Dodo went three times a week to the Zoo for flying lessons. The Unicorn wrote poetry. The Dodo sang to them in the evenings. Life was back to normal. Alexander said to William:

'Was that a nine-day wonder?'

'Yes,' said William. He was sitting back with a kipper and a cigar and a piece of Madeira cake, with his braces off, which meant he was in a mood for explaining.

'I still don't know what that means.'

'It means there is nothing so marvellous people can't get used to it.'

'Oh,' said Alexander.

They had sardines for supper, just the two of them, like old times. Alexander said it was AGES since he'd had sardines. It was a lovely evening. The sky over the Park was pink. Mrs Banyana came in in a silver dress and told Alexander a story. Alexander said:

'The Unicorn told me he'd take me to the Land of Mog when I'm big enough.'

'And when will that be?'

'Suddenly. When he knows. Is it real? Is there really a Land of Mog?'

'Oh yes,' she said. She looked very beautiful in the starlight and happy and sad at once.

'Have you been there?'

'It's the only place in the whole world I haven't been.'

'Is it far? Where is it?'

'It's where you find it.' She kissed him on

both cheeks and then on his nose. 'And now you go to sleep.'

The Dodo, who was sitting at the head of the bed, as he did every night till Alexander went to sleep, yawned, rang his bell and began to sing:

> 'It's here and there
> It's everywhere
> You'll find it anywhere.'

Just as he was falling asleep Alexander thought he heard big wheels going down the road from Piccadilly Circus to Hyde Park Corner. They seemed to go on and on and then, in the quiet afterwards, he dreamed of the Land of Mog. Then suddenly he said to himself in a cross voice:

'You're only dreaming.'

Something had woken him up.

He thought he would never get to the Land of Mog, where the Unicorn's friend and enemy, the Lion, lived.

Feet were running up and down the corridor.

He thought in his dream he had heard a lion roar. GEROOOOOO!

He looked out of the window. Lights were going on everywhere.

He would have liked to go to sleep again, but the dream was lost.

William came in in his pyjamas and said:

'The Unicorn and the Dodo have disappeared!'

Mrs Banyana came in wearing a beautiful black dress. Everyone in the hotel was very worried because the Unicorn and the Dodo had disappeared. Porters and under-porters stood to attention. Bell boys rang all the bells. Princesses, who had been dreaming of crowns they had lost, came out into the corridor in their curlers. They fainted and cried and made noises like the monkeys in Alexander's dream.

They all assembled in the ballroom. The chef made cups of tea for everyone. Alphonse served them, crying into a big silk handkerchief. The Manager put on his top hat, even though it was indoors. William put his arm round Alexander and said:

'Never mind, old chap, we'll find them, if it's the last thing we do.'

Mrs Banyana made a speech. Everyone clapped and cried. A policeman arrived with a notebook.

William said:

'Back to bed, old mate.' But Alexander could see he was worried, because he blew his nose hard, like a trumpet, into his red and white spotted handkerchief.

'I told them,' said Mrs Banyana, 'they must never, NEVER, go out without Alexander or William.'

The policeman wrote down everything everyone said. He took statements and fingerprints and photographs. He asked for pictures of the Unicorn and the Dodo. Alphonse brought in eggs and bacon and very strong tea. Then everyone went to bed.

6

Alexander woke up the next morning knowing that something was the matter. Then he remembered. Because he was brave he did not cry but tried hard to think where the Dodo and the Unicorn might have gone. He was glad because this was the first day of the school holidays and he had the whole summer, six weeks and two days, to find them.

That morning everyone was running about with a separate Plan, and they were all bumping into each other, saying 'Excuse Me', and 'I Think I've Got an Idea', and 'Something rather Urgent has just Come Up'.

In the kitchen the chef was sitting crying with his apron over his head.

In the bedrooms the Princesses were ringing bells and sobbing and sighing. But no one came to bring them breakfast or get them up or do their hair or listen to their stories about the crowns they had lost.

In his office the Manager was talking on six telephones at once.

In the garden the gardeners were cutting roses for lunch and pruning the cabbages, they were so upset.

In the corridors the bell boys were playing leap-frog to take their minds off things, while the Princesses rang and rang.

In the hall the porters were sitting sunk in gloom on the luggage which should have been sent to the railway station and the airport, to go to America and India and places even William had never heard of. The porters were so sunk in gloom they did not look up when a famous film star arrived in a big white car with a hundred suitcases, fifty trunks, twelve golf bags, six fishing rods and a yacht. He walked through the hall dropping money, followed by his private secretary and his private secretary's private secretary and his producer and his director. But still the porters were sunk in gloom.

'What's going on here?' said the famous film star. 'I thought this was the best hotel in the whole world.'

The porters said: 'The Unicorn and the Dodo have disappeared.'

'Oh,' said the famous film star, 'that is the most terrible thing I have ever heard in the whole of my life.'

By lunch time everyone was in the ballroom. They were all talking at the same time and the noise was APPALLING.

'It's such a MUDDLE,' said Alexander.

William said: 'If we all talk at once we shall never find the Dodo and the Unicorn. We must have a MEETING.'

Everyone clapped him and sat down quietly on gold chairs. Alphonse wheeled in five hundred ham sandwiches with mustard and watercress.

'There are times,' said Mrs Banyana, looking beautiful and brave, 'when I'm very proud of William.'

William was chairman. Alexander was made secretary and given a big blue notebook with lines and a red pen.

William proposed, and everyone agreed, that the first thing they should do was to make a list of things to do. This was the list just as it was written down in Alexander's notebook:

LIST OF THINGS TO DO

1. Make a list of things to do.
2. Send a telegram to Mr Banyana.
3. Send out a search party.
4. Elect a committee to decide where the search party should go.

('Excuse me,' said Alexander. 'Shouldn't that be the other way round?' 'Quite right, Mr Secretary,' said William. Everyone clapped. Alexander blushed.)

5. Find the Dodo and the Unicorn.

The committee was chosen unanimously and given badges so that everyone would know who they were. They were William, Alexander, Mrs Banyana, the Manager and the Chief of Police, who was wearing his full dress uniform. Also the President of the Magic Circle (who was rather confusing because he kept vanishing and appearing, sometimes with rabbits in his pocket), and the Dodo's flying instructor, who was the Keeper of the Eagles at the Zoo.

They all went upstairs to the Banyanas' house and Mrs Banyana put on her special committee hat. This was very big and covered in roses. They all shook hands with each other and William made a short speech:

'It is times like this,' he said, 'that bring out the Best in people.'

Mrs Banyana said: 'I shall fly, if necessary, to the ends of the earth.'

The Chief of Police said: 'No effort shall be spared.'

The Dodo's Flying Instructor, who was very thin with long arms and looked rather like a bird, said in a high, fast voice: 'Well, they're not at the Zoo, I've looked. Though you are welcome, of course, to my opinion.' Before anyone could ask him, he went on: 'Didus ineptus is a fowl of the order Columbidae. Its cranium is exceptionally small and its pennae are absurd. It is mostly extinct.'

Mrs Banyana gave him a look.

Alexander whispered to William: 'What does he mean?'

William said: 'He means that the Dodo can't fly.'

'We knew that,' said Alexander.

They turned to ask the President of the Magic Circle what he thought about the Unicorn, but he had disappeared. In his place was a bowl of goldfish, a rabbit and a bunch of roses.

'He's not much use,' said William, 'until he comes back.'

Alexander said: 'All *I* want is to find the Dodo and the Unicorn.'

They sent a telegram to Mr Banyana. They put FASTEST and MOST URGENT and TOP PRIORITY, but Mrs Banyana said it couldn't reach him till October.

They put a notice in *The Times*. Alexander wrote most of it, except the spelling, and was quite proud. It said:

> MISSING. One singing Dodo
> mostly extinct and Unicorn answer-
> ing to Your Grace. Finder will be
> REWARDED.

Just as the sun was sinking they set out: Mrs Banyana in her pink mini car, wearing a search-ing hat with goggles and radio-telephone, William and Alexander on the tandem bicycle, the Chief of Police on a big black horse with a white plume, the Keeper of the Eagles on a bus, the Famous Film Star in his big car with

only five trunks and fifty suitcases. And running to keep up with them the half of the President of the Magic Circle which had reappeared, carrying his rabbit, the bowl of goldfish and a bunch of roses. The Manager had to stay behind to look after the Princesses who had had nothing to eat all day but five hundred ham sandwiches with mustard and watercress.

Soon William and Alexander and Mrs Banyana had left everyone else behind. They stopped at last somewhere in Sussex at the top of a hill from which they could see for miles and miles, if only the sun hadn't gone down.

Mrs Banyana took off her searching hat and William fried some sausages. They felt very quiet and sad.

Alexander said: 'Perhaps we didn't believe in them enough.'

William said: 'Don't you worry. They'll turn up.'

Mrs Banyana said: 'In Tibet your father will just be getting up. He will be having his early morning cup of tea.'

'That's a good idea,' said William. And he put the kettle on.

7

In the morning Mrs Banyana said:

'I think we would do better if we split up. We should deploy our resources. I shall drive very fast in my pink mini car and if that fails I shall fly to the ends of the earth.'

'But if you drive very fast,' said Alexander, 'you might not see them.'

'On the other hand,' his mother replied, 'if I drive very slowly I might not catch them up.'

'Oh,' said Alexander.

After kippers for breakfast, cooked by William on a charcoal fire until they were absolutely delicious, Mrs Banyana kissed Alexander, shook hands with William, put on her searching hat and drove off.

They were on top of the Sussex downs. From here they could see the fields and the woods and miles and miles away the shining sea. Behind them was a ring of trees full of little eyes: rabbits and birds. It was so lovely they could almost forget about the Dodo and the Unicorn.

'What shall we do next?' said Alexander.

'Hush,' said William. He was sitting very still with his eyes closed, as if he were trying to remember something.

'Why?' said Alexander.

'Because this is a very old place and sometimes in old places you can hear things.'

Alexander sat down beside him, and whispered:

'What sort of things?'

'Voices and messages and mysteries.'

'Can you hear anything now?'

'A bit. Old Britons making their spears from these flints to fight the Romans who came from the sea.'

'Did they really? Who won?'

'The Romans. They built a temple here, where the trees are. That's like a church. If you screw up your eyes when the sun shines, you can still see it.'

'But that's history,' said Alexander. 'You can't *hear* history.'

'You can if you listen. But there are older   52

things than history here. Spirits that lived in trees and stones. The old gods, the ones the Unicorn would know. Maybe Pan.'

'Who was Pan?'

'A friend of the Unicorn's. Half horse, half man. He was the only god who died. So some say, but the Unicorn says not.'

'I bet he didn't die. I bet he went to the Land of Mog.'

'Maybe he did.' William opened his eyes, got up and brushed his coat. 'Well this won't get the baby bathed.'

He started to collect the pots and pans. He dug a hole and buried the kipper bones. Alexander was definitely going to help him but he was still thinking:

'If you can get messages can't you ask about the Dodo and the Unicorn?'

'There's too much worry in the air. There may be a message, but it can't get through.'

All day they rode their tandem bicycle. The grass was very tall and full of buttercups. William broke off a piece of honeysuckle from the hedge and put it in his buttonhole. In the fields on either side of the road lambs jumped about on springs. Sheep, who are very stupid, thought the tandem was a dangerous animal and rushed around fussing after their children. The lambs bleated MAMA but went on springing.

'Can't we ask them?' said Alexander.

'No,' said William. 'They wouldn't know and if they knew they'd have forgotten before they remembered.'

'Oh,' said Alexander.

They asked a cow. The cow allowed them to feed it some long juicy grass, munched, closed its eyes and went to sleep.

'That's cows for you,' said William.

They asked an intelligent-looking horse who was standing with his head over a gate.

'Have you seen, by any chance,' said William, 'a horse with a horn?'

'You mean a cow,' said the horse. 'There are absolutely HUNDREDS in the field next door. They do nothing but MOO MOO MOO from morning till night. They're driving me MAD.'

'No,' said William. 'A horse with a horn.'

'There's no such thing,' said the horse crossly. 'Don't be ABSURD.'

They rode through a town with a cathedral.

They rode through sleepy villages past houses with beams like eyebrows and windows like eyes. They rode through Partridge Green and Dragon's Green and Bear Green and Pease Pottage and Summer-under-the-Hill. At Summer-under-the-Hill they were so tired they propped up the tandem bicycle and sat on a bench outside a teashop to drink lemonade and eat honey cake. (Honey cake was the ONLY sweet thing that Alexander liked.)

William said: 'They're not at Partridge Green or Dragon's Green or Bear Green.'

'No,' said Alexander. 'And the cows didn't know, or the sheep or the horse.'

William said: 'They're not at Pease Pottage or Summer-under-the-Hill.'

'I don't think we'll ever find them,' sighed Alexander.

'Well it's a nice quiet afternoon,' said William. Then they went to sleep.

They woke up suddenly. A noise was approaching through a cloud of dust. People came out of the cottages and rubbed their eyes. All the dogs barked and the cocks crowed.

First came a big red lorry playing a tune like an ice-cream van. Then three caravans, then two cages on wheels. One cage was covered with a heavy tarpaulin. In the other two big lions said: 'GEROOO!'

On one lorry clowns were turning somersaults.

On another a big man, like a giant, was blowing flames out of his mouth.

Two big dappled horses came up behind with girls in silver skirts dancing on their backs.

On the side of every lorry and every cage and every caravan it said in curly letters:

THE MOST FAMOUS CIRCUS IN THE WHOLE WORLD

The dancing girls and the giant and the clowns threw leaflets into the crowd. One fell at Alexander's feet. It said:

THE MOST FAMOUS CIRCUS IN THE WHOLE WORLD

WILL BE PERFORMING

FOR ONE NIGHT ONLY

AT SUMMER-UNDER-THE-HILL

One chance only to see

GOGO the fire-eater

CHARLIE the clown
SYLVIE the bearded lady
AND MANY OTHER ATTRACTIONS
INCLUDING A SURPRISE!
Adults 12½p.
Children 4p.

Alexander said: 'I've never been to the circus.'

William said: 'As it happens, neither have I.'

They both had the same thought. They were so excited they couldn't look at each other.

William said: 'It stands to reason.'

Alexander said: 'Why didn't we think of that before?'

They had a wash and a boiled egg and a cup of tea. William put on a false beard and a Balaclava helmet Lily had knitted, and said:

'I am going to scout round. If the Dodo and the Unicorn have been stolen I shall find them.'

Alexander said: 'You're very brave, William.'

William said Alexander must come later and buy a ticket. No one would notice him because everyone expected children to go to a circus.

William spoke to Mrs Banyana on the radio telephone and explained what he was going to do. He gave Alexander 9d. for his ticket and a five-pound note just in case.

They shook hands. William went off. Alexander felt rather lonely. Then he thought of William in danger and the Dodo and the Unicorn. He remembered that his father was an explorer and his mother was famous. At eight o'clock exactly he was sitting in the circus tent. The trumpets sounded. The drums rolled. The ring-master announced THE MOST FAMOUS CIRCUS IN THE WHOLE WORLD. Alexander held his breath till he nearly burst and thought that this was the most exciting thing that had ever happened to him in the whole of his life.

8

First came the elephants holding each others' tails, walking on their hind legs and dying for the Queen. Then Gogo the fire-eater, Charlie the Clown who put his head in the lion's mouth while it was in the middle of saying 'GEROOO', and Sylvie the Bearded Lady. The Most Daring Man on the Flying Trapeze hung by his teeth without a safety net. The drums rolled. The ring-master cracked his whip. Everyone said 'OOOOH!' and 'AAAAH!'

Alexander was so excited he almost forgot about William in danger.

He almost forgot about the Dodo and the Unicorn until the drums rolled again, the trumpets trumped, the ring-master cracked his whip and on they came.

The Unicorn looked magnificent. He was dressed in silver bells and he was stamping and snorting and rolling his eyes. The Dodo waddled slowly after, stood still in the spotlight and cried and cried.

The ring-master announced:

'THE MOST FAMOUS CIRCUS
IN THE WHOLE WORLD
PRESENTS
THE MYTHICAL UNICORN
AND THE DODO
MOSTLY EXTINCT'

The crowd said: 'O O O O H!' and 'A A A A H!'

A lady in a spangled dress held up a perch for the Dodo. It blinked, climbed on and fell off, bashing its beak.

The Unicorn pranced twice round the ring, stamped, snorted and rolled its eyes. Then it turned the ring-master into a toad.

William came on wearing a black beard and a Balaclava helmet, riding a lion. The drums weren't sure whether to roll or not. The seals laughed and clapped their flippers. The lions said 'GEROOOO'. Gogo the fire-eater had hiccups. The bearded lady thumped him on the back and flames came out of his ears. The ring-master hopped around the ring trying not to get trodden on. The crowd squealed and the lights went out.

Alexander ran and ran. It was very confusing outside in the dark with all the tents and lorries and cages and caravans. Once he thought he heard someone say 'HELP'. And he thought he saw the Unicorn flash past, then a dreadful snorting and kicking. Something behind him said 'GEROOOO'. He fell over and saw he was looking at a pair of feet. A voice said 'GOTCHER!' He looked up and saw he had been caught by the most enormous man he had ever seen in the WHOLE of his life. The man had him by one ear and was saying 'HO HO'.

'Who are you?' Alexander tried to make his voice brave and firm but it wobbled a bit.

'I am Mr Jolly Brown, the owner of the Most Famous Circus in the Whole World.'

'Oh,' said Alexander. The next thing he knew he was sitting on some straw in a cage with William, the Dodo and the Unicorn. The Unicorn's horn was crumpled. The Dodo was crying so much everyone was getting wet.

'Well,' said the Unicorn. 'Look who's here.' He waved a hoof in a sarcastic sort of way.

The Dodo flapped its little wings but was crying too much to speak.

Alexander said: 'I *am* sorry. But at least we've found you.'

William said: 'Everything will look different in the morning.'

The Unicorn snorted. The Dodo began to sing:

> 'It's never so bad
> It can't be badder.
> It's never so sad
> It can't be sadder.'

In the morning the circus left Summer-under-the-Hill before anyone in the village was up. Alexander, William, the Dodo and the Unicorn were still in the cage and Mr Jolly Brown had put in a small lion as well. This was to make sure that they did not call out for help. If they did the lion would say 'GEROOO' and warn Mr Jolly Brown. Whenever they stopped Mr Jolly Brown came and rubbed his hands and said 'HO HO'. The monkeys threw banana skins into the cage. Children pointed at them and said 'OOOH' and 'AAAAH'. Once an aeroplane, that might have been Mrs Banyana's, passed overhead. A big white car that could have been the film star's swept past. But they did not dare to wave or call out because of the lion. The lion growled quietly most of the time as if it were practising to say 'GEROOOO'.

William said: 'Stone walls do not a prison make, nor iron bars a cage.'

'But they do,' said Alexander. He asked the Unicorn: 'Can't you do some magic?'

'My magic is in my horn,' said the Unicorn. 'And it's crumpled.'

Just then a red helicopter appeared buzzing on the horizon like a cross mosquito.

'It's my father!' cried Alexander.

'If he's going to save us,' said William, 'we will have to keep that lion quiet.'

Alexander, who could only just stop himself jumping up and down, said: 'I've had an idea.' He told William, who shook his head and then said:

'You are a very brave boy.' They shook hands. William wiped his eyes with his red spotted handkerchief. Even the Unicorn was impressed. The Dodo watched with big damp eyes the size of soup bowls.

Alexander walked up to the lion and said politely:

'Excuse me but you have just swallowed a fly.'

The lion opened its mouth and Alexander put his head in. The helicopter came lower, hovered and was just about to fly away. William shouted and waved his red spotted handkerchief. The Unicorn stamped and snorted. The Dodo squeaked. The lion tried to say 'GEROOO'. But his mouth was too full of Alexander.

William was busy cutting the tow rope that tied them to the lorry in front. The red helicopter came back and lowered two enormous grappling hooks. William fixed them to the bars and the whole cage was whisked up into the air. The lion was so astonished it dropped Alexander but forgot to say 'GEROOOO'.

Down below Mr Jolly Brown waved his fist. The seals barked. The monkeys chattered and the fire-eater blew out flames. But all in vain. The cage was carried over hills and valleys, over villages and towns, till it was dropped down on the roof of the famous Ritz-Palace hotel.

Everyone came up to cheer, even the Princesses, who had quite forgotten about their lost crowns.

The Chief of Police galloped up Piccadilly on his black horse with the white plume.

Just at that moment the Keeper of the Eagles got off a number 38 bus, and was nearly, but not quite, knocked down by the famous film star in his big white car.

The President of the Magic Circle vanished and reappeared half a dozen times he was so excited. Once he forgot the rabbit, the bunch of roses and the bowl of goldfish, and had to go back for them.

A silver aeroplane flew over the hotel and wrote in the sky:

THE DODO AND THE UNICORN ARE HOME AGAIN!

Everyone knew who that was, because no one but Mr Banyana would be allowed to fly so low over the famous Ritz-Palace hotel.

Someone sawed off the padlock, and the Dodo and the Unicorn, William and Alexander were free. Mr Banyana stepped out of the helicopter, curling his black moustache and smiling. He kissed Alexander and shook hands with William. He said to Alexander:

'I cannot stay long because I have to discover something in the terrible Gobi desert. But I am *very* proud of you. You are the bravest boy in the whole world.'

The Dodo tried to hug Alexander, but his wings were too short, so Alexander hugged him instead.

Everyone cheered and clapped and then they sang: 'For He's a Jolly Good Fellow!' Alexander was quite embarrassed.

The lion, who had kept its paws over its eyes all the time they were flying, opened them and said 'gerooo' in a *very* small voice. Then he went to live at the Zoo.

The silver plane circled and came back. Everyone looked up and the Dodo nearly fell backwards off the roof. Mr Banyana wagged the wings of the plane, then wrote in the sky:

ALEXANDER IS THE
BRAVEST BOY IN
THE WHOLE WORLD
AND NOW IT IS TIME
FOR EVERYONE
TO GO TO BED

9

After the Dodo and the Unicorn had come home again everything was quiet for a while. The Unicorn's horn uncrumpled. He said that if Mr Jolly Brown would agree to be good for ever and ever, he *might* turn the ring-master back from a toad. Mr Jolly Brown came to see them at the Ritz-Palace hotel, looking very sheepish. He didn't say 'HO HO' once. The Chief of Police wanted to put him in prison but he promised to be good for ever and ever. He brought the ring-master in a shoe-box with holes in the top and the Unicorn changed him back. William cooked some kippers for tea and they all became quite good friends. Mr Jolly Brown said that Alexander could come to his circus, any time he liked, for the rest of his life, without paying.

The Unicorn had become rather nicer since their terrible adventure. He was still sarcastic sometimes, but more helpful. He didn't always sigh when the Dodo sang. And he told Alexander some very interesting stories about how the world was made and the Land of Mog, and how he fought the Lion for the crown.

'He was quite a decent fellow really,' said the Unicorn. 'Still is I suppose. We simply fell out, as beasts will, but we fell in again all right. There's a picture of him on the marmalade jar. *Not* his best profile.'

Alexander looked at the marmalade jar and, sure enough, there was a splendid picture, in gold, of the Lion and the Unicorn, holding up a shield and a crown. Secretly, Alexander thought that the Lion looked superb, but he was too sensible to say so.

'What does "By appointment" mean?' he asked.

'It means,' said the Unicorn, rather grandly, 'that whenever the Lion or I wish to see the Queen, all we have to do is make an appointment.'

'I thought it meant,' said Alexander, 'that the Queen eats marmalade.'

'Many people make the same mistake,' said the Unicorn. He went out looking huffy. There was a time when he would have stamped and snorted and rolled his eyes.

'I think,' said Alexander to William, 'that he's getting nicer.'

The Dodo said: 'Underneath he has a heart of gold. You simply have to find it. It must be quite a strain being mythical.'

'That's as maybe,' said William, who was in his breakfast-eating no-talking mood.

Then two exciting things happened.

The first thing was to do with the Dodo. Alexander had been taking him every day to the Zoo for his flying lessons. On the first day they decided to go by Underground. They were a bit worried by a notice that said:

PETS MUST BE CARRIED

'I don't think I could carry you,' said Alexander.

'It's all right,' said the ticket collector. 'He's not a pet, he's a Dodo.'

The Dodo was so proud he tried to go down the up escalator. Then he tried to go up the down escalator. Then he got stuck in the automatic doors of the train. Then he went to sleep and Alexander couldn't wake him up, so they went round and round the circle line for a whole day. When they got home, very tired and hungry, William cooked them sausages and nut cutlets for the Dodo and said:

'I think next time you'd better go by bus.'

So they went every morning to the Zoo by bus. The Keeper of the Eagles took his job as the Dodo's Flying Instructor very seriously. He was rather excitable and cried sometimes or ran around waving his long thin arms. The Dodo watched with his big eyes like damp soup bowls. Then he climbed on to a box, flapped his little wings like the Flying Instructor and jumped. This was the moment when the eagles laughed, quite rudely, and Alexander covered his eyes. Because the Dodo always fell, just like a big feathered stone, and bent his beak.

'Never mind,' said Alexander, 'you'll do it next time.'

The eagles laughed. The Flying Instructor cried. The Dodo said:

'That's why I'm mostly extinct.'

The Flying Instructor said they would have to give up. The Dodo practised secretly at

night. Alexander could hear him in the airing

cupboard, jumping off the shelf and landing with a horrible THUD.

The Dodo got quite desperate. William found him one night on the balcony ledge outside the Manager's office. They had to get the fire brigade to fetch him down.

On the morning of the last lesson the Dodo was a pitiful sight. His beak was wrapped up in a bandage. Because he had had no sleep for nights he kept dropping off. He had lost a lot of feathers falling out of trees.

He climbed up a ladder to the top of the flying platform. The eagles giggled. The Dodo looked suddenly fierce and proud. The Flying Instructor went down on his knees. Alexander held his breath.

One, two, three, four, FLY!

The Dodo flapped his little wings. WHIRR WHIRR they went, until he was quite out of breath. But nothing happened. The eagles sniggered.

One, two, three, four, FLY!

The Dodo flapped his little wings and puffed out his chest. WHIRR WHIRR WHIRR went his wings, but just as he seemed about to take off, he looked down and felt dizzy. It was

so far to the ground. He covered his eyes with his wings and the eagles sneered and passed remarks.

'Last chance,' said the Flying Instructor.

One, two, three, four, FLY!

The Dodo flapped his wings, puffed out his chest and closed his eyes. WHIRR WHIRR WHIRR WHIRR went his wings. He jumped, seemed about to fall, then FLEW! Not far, but enough, the Flying Instructor said, to get his licence. The Dodo was so excited he called for a taller platform and flew again. Then he climbed a high tree and flew again. This time he fell on his beak. They carried him home on a stretcher, bandaged all over from head to claw, but the happiest Dodo in the WHOLE world. He sang, inside his head, for he could not get his voice out because of the bandages:

'It's quite absurd
I'm really a bird
Now I can fly
No need to cry.'

Then he put his head where his wing would be, if it hadn't been wrapped up in bandages, and went to sleep for a week.

10

The second exciting thing happened to the Unicorn. It happened to everyone really, but it started with the Unicorn.

After his flying accident the Dodo had his wings in splints for about a fortnight. When they were taken off he was delighted to find that he could still fly. Not very far, but he was quite happy with the distance from the airing cupboard shelf to the floor. Everyone made a great fuss of him and lots of people came to see him. People came from America and Russia and all over the world. They took photographs of him, and measured him, and wrote big books about him. He still cried a bit sometimes, but only because he was happy and rather shy.

The Unicorn, although he was pleased about the Dodo, got bored and huffy because no one wanted to interview *him* any more.

Then one morning at breakfast time a

Splendid Person arrived at the Ritz-Palace hotel. He wore a gold tail-coat, a powdered wig and silk stockings. He rode a beautiful shining bicycle and carried his nose so high in the air that Alexander, who opened the door, had to cough before he was seen by the Splendid Person.

The Splendid Person said: 'I have a message for His Grace, the Unicorn.'

Alexander took the message and said: 'Thank you, sir.'

The Splendid Person bowed and rode away, right down the middle of Piccadilly. When they saw him all the cars had to get out of the way, for no one would have dreamed of honking at such a Splendid Person.

The message said:

HIS GRACE, THE UNICORN,
IS REQUESTED TO TAKE TEA
THIS AFTERNOON WITH
HER MAJESTY THE QUEEN
AT EXACTLY FOUR O'CLOCK
BY APPOINTMENT

'But you've often been to the Palace,' said Alexander.

'This is special,' said the Unicorn. 'I feel it in my horn.'

When he got back everyone said: 'Well?' and 'What happened?' and Alexander said: 'What did you have for tea?'

The Unicorn kept them waiting a bit, and when they were nearly bursting with curiosity, he said:

'The Queen has to go to the ends of the earth on matters of State. She has asked me to look after the crown and the country while she is away.'

This was the beginning of the most exciting time. The next day the Unicorn had a special crown made for him (the Queen's was too big) and gave a garden party at the Palace just for Alexander, William, the Dodo and Mrs Banyana. Lily was asked, but decided to watch on television instead.

They had ice-cream and chocolate cake for Mrs Banyana, kippers for William, sardines for Alexander, celery for the Unicorn and nuts for the Dodo. They sent a parcel round to Lily's

afterwards with treats for her and Buster.

Afterwards they danced for a bit, then the Unicorn said:

'I'd better see how Parliament's getting on.'

They all climbed into the Queen's golden coach. Several Splendid Persons bowed so low they banged their noses on the ground. The crowds cheered and waved flags. The Dodo's eyes got bigger and bigger, bigger even than soup bowls. He waved his little wing. The Unicorn nodded, first one side and then the other. Mrs Banyana threw kisses. The sentries saluted, then were so overcome by how handsome the Unicorn looked that they dropped their bayonets and clapped.

They drove down the Mall, through Trafalgar Square and up Whitehall to the Houses of Parliament.

The Unicorn marched in looking every inch a monarch. The Dodo waddled after. The trumpeters, who had run before the carriage all the way from the Palace, blew their trumpets and the Dodo jumped and fell over. A kind policeman picked him up.

Parliament was in an AWFUL mess.

In the House of Lords all the lords were

asleep. Every one of them was snoring and some of the oldest lords in dusty corners had cobwebs growing over their faces.

'Should we wake them up?' whispered Alexander.

'No,' said the Unicorn. 'Lily can come and dust them tomorrow.'

In the House of Commons no one noticed when the Unicorn came in because they were all arguing. The Government and the Opposition were throwing buns at each other. The Speaker, who was supposed to be in charge, was sobbing into his woolsack. The Prime Minister and the Leader of the Opposition were calling each other terrible names:

'Cowardy Custard!' cried the Prime Minister.

'Puppy dogs' tails!' cried the Leader of the Opposition. Then they jumped off their front benches and began to fight, rolling about all over the floor. It was a shocking scene.

'Why are they arguing?' asked Alexander.

'It's called a debate,' said the Unicorn.

'What are they debating about?'

'How many currants to put in a bun.'

Mrs Banyana said: 'It is the most disgraceful

argument I have ever seen in the WHOLE of my life.'

William said, looking stern: 'Something must be *done*!'

The Unicorn ordered the trumpeters to blow their trumpets. Then in a terrible voice he said:

'SILENCE or I shall dissolve you!'

'Is that magic?' Alexander asked William.

'No. It means he'll send them home.'

A few people had stopped arguing, but not many. When he saw the Unicorn the Speaker sobbed louder.

The Unicorn said, in an even more terrible voice:

'SILENCE or I shall turn you all into TOADS!'

Now they all stopped arguing except the Prime Minister and the Leader of the Opposition. The Prime Minister was sitting on the tummy of the Leader of the Opposition and the Leader of the Opposition was pulling out his hair. The Unicorn turned them into toads.

There was an awful silence.

Someone picked up the Prime Minister and the Leader of the Opposition and put them in

separate cardboard boxes, with holes in the top.

The Unicorn sent everyone home and told them to pick up the buns first. Then he led the way out to the golden coach. Outside the people, who had heard what had happened, were cheering and waving flags because they were all sick of the Prime Minister and the Leader of the Opposition.

'Hurray for the Unicorn!' they cried. Then they added: 'Hurray for the Dodo! Hurray for Alexander! Hurray for Mrs Banyana! Hurray for William!'

When they got back to the Palace they had tea and scrambled eggs in their dressing-gowns. The Unicorn telephoned the Queen at the ends of the earth, and she said it was quite all right, she had often wanted to do the same thing herself.

Alexander said: 'The only thing is, now you'll have to find a new Prime Minister.'

The Unicorn straightened his crown and said: 'I shall ask William to be Prime Minister.'

William, who had been holding his breath, let out a sigh. 'That is the thing I have most wanted,' he said, 'in the WHOLE of my life.'

The Dodo had dropped off, as usual at this time of day. He woke up and said: 'What? What?'

They told him. The Unicorn said:

'And you shall be Minister of Aviation because you can fly.'

The Dodo was so excited, he went straight into the airing cupboard to practise.

Then they all went to bed.

11

While the Unicorn was King they all lived in the Palace, except William, who was very busy in Downing Street. Mrs Banyana enjoyed herself because the Unicorn said as long as he was King she could be temporary Queen. When they gave audiences she sat on a smaller throne in the throne room. Apart from half a dozen assorted crowns, she had a different hat for every hour in the day: breakfast hats, lunch hats, tea hats and dinner hats.

Alexander quite liked living at the Palace, although he spent most of his days looking for the Dodo, because there were so many airing cupboards.

Everyone said that William was the best Prime Minister they had ever had. He was very kind and fair and hardly made any speeches. He did not change at all and remembered all his old friends when he chose his ministers.

The Dodo, of course, was Minister of Aviation.

The President of the Magic Circle was Chancellor of the Exchequer. William said that anyone who looked after all the country's money needed to know magic.

Mr Jolly Brown, who was quite a reformed character, was Minister of Entertainments.

Alexander was Minister of Education, at least until he went back to school. ('But my spelling isn't very good,' he said to William. 'That's all right,' William said, 'you can get someone to spell for you.')

The Keeper of the Eagles was made Chief Personal Private Confidential Secretary to the Dodo at the Ministry of Aviation.

Lily was offered the job of Minister of Cooking but said thank you very much, she'd rather not. Buster wouldn't like her going out to work. But she'd have tea ready for them when it was all over.

'Will it be all over?' Alexander asked William over kippers for breakfast at Downing Street. 'Don't you want to be Prime Minister 85 for ever and ever?'

'Enough is as good as a feast,' said William, taking another kipper.

'Is it another nine-day wonder?'

'Something like that.'

Although it only lasted for a short time, till the Queen came back from the ends of the earth, the magic reign of the Unicorn was remembered in England for ever and ever.

Never had there been such splendid parties at the Palace. Mr Jolly Brown brought his circus. The President of the Magic Circle brought his magic. There were fireworks and dancing and games. Anyone could come in without paying.

Never had there been such splendid processions. Every day, at exactly twelve o'clock, there was a procession. First came the trumpeters. Then the Unicorn and Mrs Banyana and Alexander in the golden coach (and the Dodo if he could be found in the airing cupboard). Then all the Queen's horses and all the Queen's men. Then Mr Jolly Brown's circus.

Everyone was so happy that they worked twice as hard as usual and the Bank of England was full of money. People came from all over the world to see the magic reign of the Unicorn, and the Queen sent a telegram from the ends of the earth:

YOU ARE LOOKING AFTER
THE COUNTRY VERY WELL.
WE SHALL BE BACK FROM
THE ENDS OF THE EARTH
IN ONE MONTH AT EXACTLY
FOUR O'CLOCK.

The Unicorn made a just, wise and handsome monarch. He only did magic occasionally and only turned a few people into toads. One was a wicked spy. One was a thief who tried to steal the Crown Jewels. He put them in the Palace pond with the former Prime Minister and the Leader of the Opposition. He said he would turn them back later when they had learned to be good.

Although everyone else was so happy he seemed almost sad now, he took his job so seriously. He walked round the Palace gardens with Alexander and the Dodo, and his beautiful head seemed bowed heavy beneath the crown.

'It should have been the Lion, you know.

He won in the battle for the crown a long time ago.'

Alexander said: 'But you make a very good monarch. Your magic reign will be remembered in England for ever and ever.'

The Unicorn stopped to crop a rose.

'It will not be much longer now. I should like to do something marvellous before I go.' He sighed. 'I had never realized before that magic is a responsibility.' Suddenly his mood changed. He stamped his hoof and tossed back his head, scanning the sky where the sun was setting and the moon coming up. He announced: 'I shall send a rocket to the moon. England will be proud and remember my magic reign!'

Alexander hopped up and down with excitement. 'Who will you send?'

'Ah,' said the Unicorn. 'That is the problem.'

The Dodo, who had been very quiet all this time, began to sing:

'I would like to fly
Up in the sky.
Why
Not I
?'

'He's brave,' said Alexander.

'He can fly,' said William, later.

'He is the nicest bird I have ever met in the WHOLE of my life,' said Mrs Banyana.

'He's my *best* friend,' said the Unicorn.

The Dodo was so overcome he went into the airing cupboard for a whole week. When he came out it was time to go to the moon.

On midsummer's day, the day for going to the moon, almost everyone in England came to Salisbury Plain. Mr Jolly Brown was there with his circus. The President of the Magic Circle was there some of the time when he was not vanishing with excitement. The Manager of the Ritz-Palace hotel was there, wearing his top hat and a gold chain. Even the Princesses were there, in a special coach. Mrs Banyana wore a marvellous silver evening dress, although it was morning, with a space hat. Lily watched on television. So did Buster.

At exactly eleven o'clock the Dodo finished a big breakfast of nuts and honey, put on his space suit and waddled out to the launching platform. He looked a lonely and rather peculiar little figure, much smaller than his

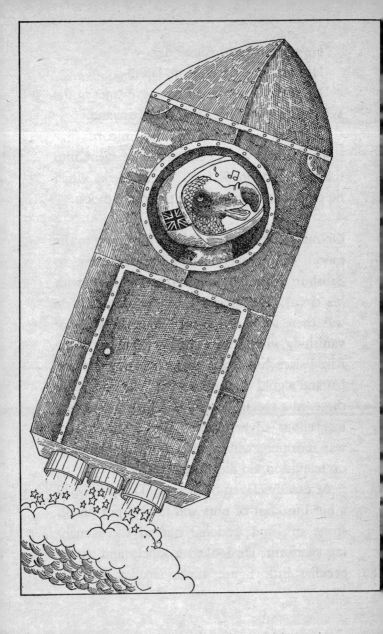

photographs in the newspapers. For days the papers had been full of the Dodo and headlines about him:

BRITISH BIRD FOR MOON
BIRDSHOT FOR BRITAIN
LUNAR LANDING FOR
DARING DODO

He didn't look very daring now. He tripped over twice on the way to the launching platform, and then fell down the ladder. The Keeper of the Eagles picked him up, dusted him and set him off again in the right direction. At the top of the ladder he turned, flapped one little wing and was gone.

Alexander was doing the count down.

FIVE FOUR

William mopped his eyes with his red spotted handkerchief and said: 'I hate to see him go.'

THREE

On their television screen they could see the Dodo lying down in his bunk. Except that it looked like an airing cupboard it was the same as any spacecraft. There was a sandwich box marked NUTS and a sandwich box marked HONEY.

The Unicorn cried, the first tear he had ever shed in the whole of his life. It rolled down his beautiful cheek, and falling into the grass was turned into a diamond and lost.

TWO ONE

The Dodo saluted, cried a bit inside his space helmet and went to sleep.

ZERO!

With a thump and a roar and a crackle the launcher was ignited. After an AWFUL minute the rocket was off. It flashed silver in the sky and got SMALLER and SMALLER and SMALLER till it was gone.

Much later that night, they could hear the Dodo singing softly to himself out among the stars:

'The stars are beautiful and bright
The moon does shine with lovely light.
I'm up above the earth so high
Like a Dodo in the sky.'

'This is the most marvellous day in the WHOLE of my life,' said Alexander.

'It will be remembered in England,' said William, 'for ever and ever.'

The Unicorn said no one need stay up. He

would know by magic if the Dodo was all right.

On Salisbury Plain the lights went out one by one. Then everyone went to bed.

12

Everyone went home to watch the Dodo's daring adventure in space on television. It took him two days to get to the moon. Most of the time he slept, sang little songs and played at being weightless. He watched with eyes like washing-up bowls as his sandwich boxes floated round and round the cabin. They had tried to make the spacecraft as much like home as possible. There were photographs of the Unicorn and Alexander on the wall and a cupboard he could go into when he got shy.

When he landed something went wrong with the television and no one could see anything. It was a very worrying time.

William mopped his forehead with his red spotted handkerchief.

Alexander said: 'I think I shall burst.'

There was a crackle and a pop and suddenly

they could hear a little voice from a long way away:

'Dodo to Unicorn. Dodo to Unicorn. Roger over.'

'Who's Roger?' asked Alexander, but no one took any notice, they were too excited.

The Dodo put on his special moon suit and waddled down the ladder. He put some bits of moon in his sandwich box, had a little nap, then planted the Union Jack. He bounced around like a rubber ball to show how easy it was to fly on the moon. And then, so sleepy he could hardly get up the ladder, he came home.

The newspapers said:

LUNAR LANDING
FOR BRAVE BIRD
BRITISH FOWL FLIES HIGH

All the important people in England started eating nuts and honey and going to the Keeper of the Eagles for flying lessons.

When the Dodo splashed down in the Palace pond it was a day that England would remember for ever and ever. The sun was shining and all the bells of London crashed in the blue sky, fit to burst.

Everyone came to the Palace.

All the people of London came and sang: 'For He's a Jolly Good Dodo.'

The Keeper of the Eagles came. Mr Jolly Brown came with his circus. He had bathed all the seals specially, and the lions had had a dry shampoo and set. The President of the Magic Circle came but was so excited he disappeared completely. The Manager of the Ritz-Palace hotel came with all the Princesses, and the bell boys, and Alphonse and the famous film star. The Chief of Police came and gave all the prisoners in England a holiday. Even the television interviewer, Mr Simon Anstruther-Pettigrew-Pringle came. He had stopped being rude and said: 'Excuse me' and 'Thank you for having me'. Lily said she would watch on television and so would Buster.

At four o'clock exactly the Queen arrived from the ends of the earth, wearing her best crown.

At half past four something buzzed on the horizon. Everyone looked up and saw a red helicopter circling the Palace garden. Mr Banyana stepped out, smiling and curling his moustache, straight from the terrible Gobi desert. He kissed Alexander and Mrs Banyana and shook hands with William. He said:

'I have come straight from the terrible Gobi desert because this is a day England will remember for ever and ever. I shall stay for a week.'

Alexander said: 'This is the HAPPIEST day in the WHOLE of my life.'

At five o'clock the Dodo splashed down. He stepped out of the pond, which was not very deep, and waddled towards the platform where the Queen was waiting with the Unicorn, Alexander, Mr and Mrs Banyana and William. She said the Unicorn could still be monarch till tomorrow because she was tired from going to the ends of the earth.

All the bells in London rang. The people of London sang 'For He's a Jolly Good Dodo'. The Dodo took off his space helmet and blinked at the crowds with eyes as big as dinner plates.

'It's quite absurd,' he said. 'I'm only a bird.'

The Queen said: 'England will remember this day for ever and ever.' And gave him a medal of the Most Noble Order of the Dodo. Since he was the only Dodo no one else could ever receive this medal. The Queen said: 'Any time you wish to see us, you need only make an appointment.'

The Dodo said: 'I have brought you back a piece of moon rock. It says MOON all the way through.' Then he bowed beautifully, just as if he met the Queen every day, stepped backwards and fell all the way down to the bottom of the steps. Then he put his head under his wing and went to sleep.

That evening there was dancing and fireworks and a feast. Alphonse had made an ice-cream as big as the Albert Hall in the shape of a Dodo. A dance was invented called the Dodo. You waddled two steps and fell over. It was quite fun, but some of the Princesses, having fallen over, could not get up. They lay like beetles waving their legs in the air.

As soon as the sun went down the fireworks were let off. There were sparklers and jumpers and bangers and wheels. And portraits of the Dodo, the Unicorn, the Queen and Alexander.

Alexander thought how marvellous it was to be famous and happy. How much he loved Mr and Mrs Banyana, William and his friends the Dodo and the Unicorn! He turned to hug the Dodo who had been sleeping all this time, but now woke up to sing:

> 'Our tale is run
>   Our song is done
>   It's time to fly
>   We must not cry
>   So good night, everyone.'

'I'm not really crying,' he said. But his big round eyes were full of tears.

William said: 'What he wants is a nice cup of tea.'

But the Dodo had already gone back to sleep.

Alexander went to look for the Unicorn. He walked through the gardens and all the rooms of the Palace. He asked the Queen's horses and the Queen's men and all the Splendid Persons. No one knew where the Unicorn was.

At last he found the Unicorn in the throne room, in the dark. He was wearing his purple cloak and his crown and he was sitting on the best throne, which was still his until tomorrow. He seemed to glow in the dark and at first Alexander thought he was asleep. Then there was a great sigh, like the rustling of stars, if stars could rustle.

Alexander sat on the bottom step of the throne and pressed his face against the purple cloak.

'You won't leave us, will you? Ever?'

'Alas,' said the Unicorn, 'it is time to go.'

'Why?'

The Unicorn said with a gentleness Alexander had never before heard in his voice:

'Because I am losing my magic. Because it is time to go back to the old place and walk again with friends and enemies.'

'The Lion?' asked Alexander, in a whisper.

'And others.'

'How will you get there?'

'I have enough magic. It is failing, but enough to take us.'

'Will you take me?'

'Later perhaps, when my magic is renewed in the Land of Mog. I have walked too long on the earth.'

'Will you come for me?'

'Yes. When it is the time.' The Unicorn brushed Alexander's head with his hoof. He lifted the crown from his head and laid down

the sceptre and the orb. He flung off the purple cloak.

The Dodo waddled in, rubbing his eyes with his wings:

'Is it time to go?'

'Yes.'

Alexander said, as bravely as he could: 'Yours has been a magic reign. They will remember for ever and ever.'

He hugged the Dodo and shook the Unicorn by the hoof. It was a solemn occasion.

'Will you be all right in the Land of Mog?'

'There will be a reckoning,' said the Unicorn, 'with the Lion, about the crown. And many perils, magic and mystery. You are a brave boy, and kind. You have believed in us. Your time will come for the Land of Mog.'

The Unicorn knelt down on all fours. The Dodo climbed on his back and they walked to the window above the rose garden. The party was still going on and only Alexander saw them fly away. The Unicorn glowed white in the sky, tossed his horn and kicked up his hoofs, spilling a shower of sparks and stars. Then he was gone.

Alexander stood for a long time at the window, waving, even after they had disappeared into the Milky Way. Then he went to look for William.

Alexander looked often for the Unicorn and the Dodo in the sky, but he knew really that they were not in the space you can see from earth. The Land of Mog was far beyond the stars and only magic could reach it.

Before he left, the Unicorn turned the toads back into people and William stopped being Prime Minister.

The day after the happiest day in his life Alexander thought it was nice to be back home again in the house on top of the Ritz-Palace hotel.

'I quite liked being famous,' he said to William, 'but now can we go to Lily's for tea?'

About the author

Janice Elliott writes: 'Just before my first novel was due to be published in 1962 I left London and the Sunday Times to move to Sussex and concentrate on writing novels, living in a 16th-century cottage.

'This is my first children's book. It took about three weeks to write, and I found it one of the most exciting and satisfying things I have ever done. I wrote it, of course, for my son, Alexander. He later asked for a sequel – and *Alexander in the Land of Mog* is now published in hardback by Brockhampton.'

Janice Elliott is also well known as a writer of novels for adults, but hopes to be able to write more books for children. Her main hobby is sailing with her husband and Alexander.

Worzel Gummidge and Saucy Nancy

Barbara Euphan Todd

'I've always had a fancy to see the sea,' remarked Worzel when he heard John and Susan were to have their holiday at the seaside instead of Scatterbrook Farm. 'Maybe Earthy and me might come along the day arter tomorrow. Oooh Aye! Seaside, that's the name o' the place, ain't it?'

But the name of the place was Seashell, which had never entertained a pair of scarecrows before, and from the goings on that followed their arrival, it would never want to again. Mrs Bloomsbury-Barton was absolutely horrified by the song Saucy Nancy, the ship's figurehead, sang in her bath, and no-one was pleased when Earthy 'tidied up' all the clothes on the beach.

Charlotte Sometimes

Penelope Farmer

Imagine going off to boarding school for the first time and waking up to find you are in the same school, but everything else in the room has changed, you are called by a new name and are in fact a different girl living in the same school forty years earlier. Not only that but you keep switching backwards and forwards, being yourself and making friends and doing lessons in today's world and waking up for no reason to different friends and lessons right in the middle of World War One.

No wonder Charlotte got tired and confused and into trouble for calling her headmistress by the wrong names and forgot to tell her other self about the girl who was supposed to be her best friend.

Charlotte you see was only Charlotte Sometimes, and however interesting it was to have two selves, she really preferred being herself.

For everyone over ten but girls may enjoy it most.

Bottersnikes and Gumbles

S. A. Wakefield

Deep in the Australian bush , where the Spiny Anteater and the Kookaburra live, there are some even more unusual animals – Bottersnikes and Gumbles. Bottersnikes are ugly. They have green faces with slanting eyes, noses like cheesegraters, mean little mouths, and ears that turn red when they are angry, which is often and they find their homes readymade in rubbish heaps among rusty old pots and pans.

Gumbles are little creatures who love to paddle in ponds (they can't actually swim) and are hopeless when they go all giggly.

When some Bottersnikes caught some nice round little Gumbles they discovered they could squeeze them to any shape they liked without hurting them, and that if they were pressed very hard they flattened out like pancakes and couldn't get back to their proper shapes without help.

'Useful,' growled the Bottersnike King. 'We can pop 'em into jam tins and squash 'em down hard so's they can't get away, and when I want some work done they'll be ready and waiting to do it.' And so began the long, comic struggle between the Gumbles and the Bottersnikes, for the Gumbles were much too clever to stay stuck in those pesky jam tins for long.

For readers of eight and over.

The Town That Went South

Clive King

Gargoyle the rectory cat made the Discovery on his way to his night hunting grounds; where there should have been railway lines there was only cold, choppy water. Gargoyle went straight to the Vicar, who rang the church bells for everyone to gather in the square and decide what to do about The Flood.

But it wasn't a Flood. It was something even more astonishing. The town of Ramsly had come adrift from the rest of England and was floating gently across the Channel to France. By the author of *Stig of the Dump*.

For readers of eight and over,

Fattypuffs and Thinifers

André Maurois

Edmund Double loved food and was plump, like his mother, while Terry his brother could hardly wait to leave the table and was consequently very thin, like his father. Nonetheless, they were all very fond of each other and the boys were amazed when, happening by chance to take a moving staircase to the Country Under the Earth, they found themselves split up and thrust headlong into the midst of the dispute between the warring nations of the Fattypuffs and the Thinifers.

The sparkle and easy humour of André Maurois' book is certain to fascinate children of all ages as long as Fattypuffs and Thinifers co-exist and remain mutually indispensable.

Hobberdy Dick

K. M. Briggs

Long ago, long before our great-grandfathers were born and before the ancient ways left our countryside, there was plenty of secret folk life in England, particularly hobgoblins who guarded the houses and lands and watched over the families who lived in them, until their task was done and they were released. Those hobgoblins were shy folk who stayed out of sight, but they were also determined and meddlesome creatures with strong likes and dislikes.

Hobberdy Dick of Widford Manor in the Cotswolds, was a good and careful guardian but the new family who came in after the Civil War did not win his affection like the Culvers, whom he had known and liked for two hundred years.

K. M. Briggs is a well-known authority on folk lore, and Hobberdy Dick is so memorable and charming a character that this book is very well worth reading, not just for its wealth of magic and historical material but for its fascinating story.

The Minnipins

Carol Kendall

Every good Minnipin should act exactly like the others, and have the same healthy respect for the leading family, the Periods. But Muggles, she was beginning to question the smug authority of the Periods, and to sympathise more with Gummy the poet, Curley Green the painter, and Walter the Earl, the old antiquarian. So, when the eccentrics were outlawed from the village, Muggles went with them to build a new settlement high on a mountain, and for the first time in their lives they were all happy.

Then the old enemies of the Minnipin people found their way back into the Minnipin valley, but could the exiles ever make all the people in the village believe in their danger?

The Minnipins is one of those great and wise fantasies that enrich the imagination and also help us to see our own world more clearly.

A Book of Goblins

edited by Alan Garner

'The woman stood in the middle of the floor. She was dressed in white, and had white hair. She opened her eyes with a small stick, and the upper eyelid fell back over her head like a hat.

'I am two hundred and ninety winters,' she said, 'and I serve nine masters, and the house in which you stand is haunted by demons.'

This sinister old woman from the Japanese legend 'The Goblin Spider' is just one of the extraordinary beings Alan Garner has gathered in this anthology. In it you will meet such oddities as Bash Tchelik, the winged Russian demon who could overcome whole armies, and Yallery Brown, the tiny, malignant old man who brought misery on the boy who helped him, and the man of snow who wed the Red Indian chief's daughter.

For readers of ten and over.

If you have enjoyed this book and would like to know about others which we publish, why not join the Puffin Club? You will receive the club magazine, *Puffin Post*, four times a year and a smart badge and membership book. You will also be able to enter all the competitions. For details, send a stamped addressed envelope to:

The Puffin Club Dept. A
Penguin Books Limited
Bath Road
Harmondsworth
Middlesex